PRE-
HIST-
ORIC

Prehistoric

by John Paul Stadler

The Cupboard
Volume Twenty-Six
Denver | New York

The Cupboard Pamphlet
www.thecupboardpamphlet.org

Copyright ©John Paul Stadler | 2016.
All rights reserved.

ISBN 978-0-9978996-0-3

THIRD PRINTING

For Billy Byron, who always had a baby bottle and a spanking waiting for me.

CONTENTS

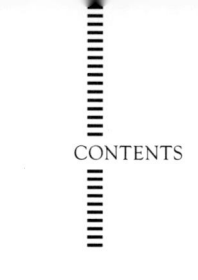

PREHISTORIC	1
BOLOGNA	3
BA DA BA BA BA	5
THE NEW WORLD	7
MOTHER'S BREAD	9
WINDMILLS	11
MUSCATATUCK	13
BINGO	15
THE BODY IN THE ROCK	17
THE LINDBERG BABY	19
APIARIAN	21
CAT THROWER	23
SHOOTING THE MOON	25
THE BALLOONIST	27
EFFIGY	29
EARTHQUAKE	31
CONFESSION	33
SLEEPWALK	35
TRANSLATION	37
THE BOOK OF SIN	39
FORT/DA	41
WALL DRUG	43

PREHISTORIC

DIAGONAL STRIATIONS—ONCE ADHERING TO annotated backs—no longer cling to our developments. These images, loosely held under sheaths of cellophane, gather gassy, shrieking babies in sepia tones, reptilian aunts speaking in tongues, boys with cowlicks slicked into submission, itinerant fathers and perpetually pregnant mothers, reunions and baptisms and weddings and everyday days bleeding into one another. In this album, death manifests in a table of macaroni casserole and ham blossoms. Our favorite recipes are missing, a recognition of absence. Anniversaries, sacraments, celebrations, and vacations—these occassions lose singularity, taking up residence just outside of time. Even still, faces sag and crows feet crinkle; raiment and hair capture each era without irony. First walks, first bicycle rides, first marriages, first ice cream cones. Last suppers, last dances, last babies, last chances. And all the in-betweens. Lost moments held captive in the leatherbound tome, a book as prehistoric as the icthyosaurus, just as exotic and unknowable, just as fleeting and bereft. The family album secrets away our past, punctuates each image with a question mark, even as it pretends to know. The dust cannot be shaken off.

BOLOGNA

OVERTURNED STONES BY THE OUTSKIRTS OF TOWN fail to complete a circumference that once led to greater depths. The scheme to belay the wishing well for pocketfulls of quarters ends in rope burn. At the bottom of the well, Joseph soothes his peeled palms in the corrugating pool. Coins plop into the shallow water or welt his chubby face, pocking his otherwise smooth skin. Over tuna casserole, we notice his absence. "He has always been rubenesque," Mother says. "The well may slim him down." No need to fret. We head to the hole in the earth and toss pebbles in. We have no coins to spare. He expectorates some incomprehensible plea; his gusto gives us hope. Mother throws down a bologna sandwich, which stifles his whimpers. With time, there is a prayer vigil and a rally and a special report and a livefeed and a nickname and a slogan and a hashtag and an interview and an article, and consequently, our family profits. Attention grows and we lose sight of an exit strategy. We mug for the cameras and speak of the travesty—our poor, trapped brother. We throw bologna sandwiches into the well and wish Joseph well. Mother cultivates a state of pre-histrionics for her well-bound boy. "Well well well," she mutters to the mirror. "Well well well." The coins accrue. Eventually, Mother passes away. Passersby say hello to the well-bound boy. Their wishes elevate Joseph's position over time. Slowly but surely, he rises. By his eighty-fourth birthday, his nose crests the rim. Bologna-fed and skinny, he tip-toes atop the pile of coins, gazing out upon the world that wished him well, and sinks back down.

BA DA BA BA BA

ONE DAY THE THISTLEWEED WILL OVERTAKE THAT sesame-crusted grave, obscuring the monthly rites we practice. Ondine's curse sings Great Aunt Claire to her rest. In death, she bequeaths to us a house of ill-tempered cats and one command: "Throw a Big Mac at my grave." This wish, written in notarized legalese—*Whereupon the first day of the month shall pass, a party to the deceased shall, by way of remittance from an endowment established by the executor of the will, procure one signature double-pattied hamburger from the nearest McDonalds fast food establishment and convey it posthaste upon the gravestone of the deceased, through velocitous aereal transmission, in loving memory of the departed*—is not one we question, knowing final wishes escape the grasp of the living. Once a month we pilgrimage from golden arches to graveyard, paper bag in hand, and, rather than plant flower or flag, hurl the double-pattied hamburger at headstone, read tarot cards, drink Miller High Life, and sunbathe. The brief visitiations provide respite from the monotomy of family life. We continue the devotional rite until the restaurant closes by decade's end. Remnants of past venerations remain, untouched by wildlife, preserved through rain and sleet and snow. Every once in a while, we find stray packets in the recesses of the station wagon. With ketchup, we stencil Ronald's blood red smile on the headstone, and in tangy barbeque sauce, the Hamburglar's caped silhouette on the back. We remember the special sauce and lettuce that ricocheted like fireworks off of the stone ediface and this is enough to curl a smile or two.

THE NEW WORLD

CLAY DENIES OUR FAMILY PLOT ITS SUMMER GARDEN after seven hard years spent tilling the land. One day we awaken and the world is red. Prehistoric red. Thick, blood-red. A patina we do not imagine in our wildest dreams. The tree trunks and limbs and leaves are red. The water red. The earth red. The sky red, the clouds red, the sun red. Reading blight and cataclysm into the blushing world, Mother passes the Lord's judgment onto us. She cuts fresh switches from the drooping sapling and thrashes us for our sins. We weep and wail and gnash our teeth. The redemptive tool crosshatches rivulets into our freckled bodies. We all cry but Saul, who chuckles at the ploy. When Mother registers his delight, she refuses him his reckoning, giving the Lord's forgiveness to us alone, a sight he laughs at. Mother blindfolds him and continues our thrashing to ransom this world. Saul smiles at the sound, bears a toothy grin. She plugs his ears with beeswax and binds his legs in rope and places him on an altar before us. We take our beating and grow redder and redder and Saul sees nothing, hears nothing, and in the new red world, disappears.

MOTHER'S BREAD

AS SHE FALLS DOWN THE STAIRS, MOTHER BAKES bread. Tumbling, she toils: rolling, leavening, kneading the dough. In her oven, loaves of pumpernickel, sourdough, and rye rise, spreading the scent of yeast and yearning through the shoe-sized house. The seven of us—her children—watch from the landing below: our arms outstretched, our mouths open. Mother, an acrobat in her younger days, rediscovers nimbleness as face meets wooden step. Halfway down the stairs, her graceful teeth abscond from their roots. Cheek bones break into prismatic rays. Joshua, the youngest, pines for the bread and holds his belly. Mother coos between bursts of blood, placating his prehistoric hunger, and sheds a tear for the pumpernickel, which she finally perfects. At the last step, her flailing arms deliver Joshua a loaf. We seven children lie atop the freshly baked bread, chewing morsel after morsel of her hardship. Mother lies at the landing, arms reaching and mouth agape, softly salivating.

WINDMILLS

Years later, the barbershop burns down, leaving prehistoric ruins that obscure its past. Father sits back in the worn leather chair and Mika, the barber woman, trims his sideburns. Like clockwork, he makes this sojourn twice a month, bringing us along, although never to get our own hair cut. He offers us a quarter to find a windmill in the cascade of magazines. My brothers and I scour the well-worn rags, never finding the lilting sails he insists are there. One Saturday my brother Joshua cheats, stowing a *National Geographic* inside his trowsers. When my father leaves us for the barber chair, Joshua reveals his contraband, the solution to this impossible task. On page eighty-seven, a windmill stands starkly among a field of poppies. "What do you think of that?" he asks us. Overjoyed, I grab the magazine from his hands and run to the back of the shop, where Mika slowly lathers my father's whisping hair in the sink. She drops the shampoo upon seeing me. I drop the windmill upon seeing her. My father starts, grabs the magazine from the floor, and, bewildered, places a quarter in my palm.

MUSCATATUCK

AFTER THE BODIES WASH ASHORE, MOTHER forbids us from visiting the Muscatatuck. My brothers and I go creek stomping there anyway, and one-by-one we are picked off by natives. My brothers scream for mercy as they meet their Maker. Peter is scalped; William is bludgeoned by a cudgel; Joseph is shot through the heart by an arrow. We place stones on their chests to bury their corpses beneath the water's trembling surface. By noon, Joshua and I are the sole survivors of the ambush. We ford the river and climb the trail to our tucked away cave, where we make a fire, eat beef jerky, and eventually fall asleep. At sunset I wake to find Joshua cradling his disarticulated head. I run from him, dizzy from the sight. The pebbles below my feet quake. Back at the Muscatatuck, I cross the rope bridge we built the day before. It shakes. The water below me burbles, collects into dewlets and droplets and precipitates toward the sky. I look to the trees; their branches lilt heavenward. "The natives are near," I whisper to no one. I hear them chant from every direction. As their warning grows, my feet lose their grip. Gravity abandons me. I grab ahold of the weeping willow's stalks so as not to leave the earth, the tree now smiling at my position. Upside down, clinging desperately to terrafirma, I look to the natives below, their machetes and blow darts poised.

BINGO

THE OCTOGENARIANS PLAY BINGO WITHOUT hearing the numbers being called. Even with their ear trumpets, they are stone deaf. It is only by fluke or premonition or muscle memory that their quivering hands daub their cards with any accuracy. We exploit their torpor with our cat-like reflexes, daubing our cards at triple their speed. So as not to raise suspicions, we conceal our age with costume and charm. We wear knickerbockers and derby caps and chew tobacco and we spit. We fit in well. But bingo here is not like bingo elsewhere. Here bingo is a rite of death (*kaput, blammo, sayonara*) where the caller reads malignant tumors and heart attacks in B-I-N-G-O and eulogies and wills in one through seventy-five. Aunt Claire dies of bingo on G-47 and I inherit her dauber. When my brothers and I win, though, we do not die. Our guises fool no one. We are immortal and we know it. We win car wash coupon books and porcelain serving platters. Prizes reserved for youth. The books we burn and the platter I drop on Thanksgiving Day, the shards piercing my arms. Mother shrieks and Father scolds. "You are a clumsy boy," they say. "Bingo!" I answer. I am sent to my room without supper, where I learn to play Chinese checkers.

THE BODY IN THE ROCK

"This prehistoric account is false," I say, slamming the textbook shut. My teacher smacks me across the back of the head with her pointing rod and I bleed. "Are we amphibians?" she asks. "Yes," I reply. This is the correct answer and my teacher knows it, but the book says we are not. "We are neither apes, nor birds, nor amphibians," she says, "We are rocks." The prehistoric primer says so. "We find people in rocks. And so people are rocks." "Rocks?" I ask. "But do rocks bleed?" She considers this question and asks me if I am bleeding. "Yes," I say. "You hit me with your rod and now I'm bleeding." "Then rocks bleed," she says. And so I discover I am rock. During recess I run to the jungle gym, making sure not to step on a crack. When I reach the playground I realize for the first time that it is covered in gravel. I ache for my ancestors as I walk on them, breaking many backs, and curse myself. At the top of the jungle gym I stop bleeding and start crying. I climb down, fill my pockets with gravel and bury these ancestors in the backyard at home. My siblings tell my parents I am burying bodies. My parents call the police. They dig up the backyard, where they find our dead cat, Yogurt, but no bodies in the rocks.

THE LINDBERG BABY

ON TUESDAY, MY PARENTS KIDNAP THE LINDBERGH baby. The neighbors stop by to greet the new arrival and offer felicitations. Mother says the boy is orphaned, the sole child of a lost relation. This shuts them up, but not the baby. Charles Jr. cries and cries until we give him a banana. With the banana in his mouth, he cries and gags and cries. At two, we baptize him Joshua, and by three he thinks he is one of us. But he is not. In a family of redheads, he is the only blonde, the only blue-eyed, the only unfreckled. We call him towhead, and when he annoys me I give him prehistoric purple nurples that last forever. In September he disappears, and we scour the countryside, posting lost ads on telephone poles. Mother grows sympathetic to Anne Morrow's melancholia. She too wants her son's safe return. We later find the boy at the Millers'. He had crossed the cow pasture on foot and sat on their stoop, eaten one bite from each slice of bread and drunk their delivered milk. We repay the Millers in boysenberry pies and bring the buck-toothed boy home. Mother beats him that night with father's belt and when we hear the howls come from below we say, "Now. Now he is one of us."

APIARIAN

My father grows a beard of bees. In the apiary he makes love to the queen and for supper we eat honeyed ham and baklava. My mother cries over cornbread, which we sprinkle with pollen. When my sister Grace grows allergic to the bee stings, she swells like a marshmallow. Father threatens to ship her off to Aunt Claire's bed and breakfast, but the droning bees lull his language to sleep. Grace writhes on the floor as we rub honey on her fattened belly. The bees continue stinging. I tell her, "This is not pain," and she nods knowingly. When I begin to grow bees on my chin, my mother cries. Father teaches me to shave in the summer with the razor his father used. The bees drop one by one into a bucket of water. The queen sees this and flees to Texas in a huff. Mother buys a heifer, and we eat yogurt and cottage cheese and drink buttermilk from then on.

CAT THROWER

MY BROTHER JOSEPH TAKES TO THROWING CATS. THIS behavior is better, we tell him, than punching holes in the wall. The cats meow spasmodically in their airborn state. After perfecting his cat throw, Joseph learns to cat-juggle, catching and releasing the tawny balls of fur by their napes. When he masters seven, we notify the press. They televise the demonstration for the five o'clock news. We train the cats to meow Beethoven's 5th while Joseph juggles them. The reporter calls the performance breathtaking, but it is not without detractors. PETA pickets the act, and the Westboro Baptist Church pickets PETA, and Hell's Angels picket Westboro, exchanging awe for outrage, sanctimony, and intimidation. For Christmas, Father buys Joseph a knife set and encourages him to add them to the act. He does so clumsily, incorporating knife after cat, knife after cat, adding twenty feet to the arc of his parabola. With this change in routine, though, not all the cats are pleased. Yogurt, the smallest kitten, bites Joseph on the wrist during the rotation. Joseph curses the cat and drops the act literally and collateral damage ensues. Today our home is littered with holes and cats who run through them, meowing half-remembered symphonies.

SHOOTING THE MOON

THE ROOM PULSATES, BUT WHEN THE SIRENS SOUND, we continue playing Euchre. I am shooting the moon. Porters rush the cabin with news of evacuation. "The *Lusitania* is sinking!" They bore us with their hysterics. No violins play, so we continue our game. I strike with the right bower and the left. An ace, a queen, a ten of spades, and I've shot it. The prehistoric moon rises as the Lusitania descends. Grace scores the hand and water thrashes against our ankles. Joseph wades in with news of our parents' departure; they are the first to jump ship. Lightning illuminates the porthole. We forget life preservers and slosh through waterlogged hallways, galoshing our way to the deck. William brings his kite. Amidst the frenzy, we replicate Franklin's experiment, shouting, "Let's go fly a kite, up to the highest height!" When lightning strikes, the charge radiates across the water's surface, electrifying all. Evacuees glare at us as they scuffle for the remaining lifeboats. We shrug our shoulders and bid them adieu. Soon the the Lusitania is ours alone. We shuffle the deck and deal the hands atop toppling tables. We play air violin, grab the five-finger discount on wine, and recite every four-letter word we know. We can do whatever we please. Saul finds a gun and shoots the moon for real. When the newspaper articles are written, there is a conspicuous silence with regard to my winning streak.

THE BALLOONIST

UNCLE HARRY ARRIVES BY BALLOON AMIDST THE crimson fall. All are dumbstruck. We don't even know we have an Uncle Harry until he shows up. It is the first time I see a man travel by hot air, but not the last. Unpacking his wares, Uncle Harry distributes souvenirs from his journeys. My brothers and I receive bananas and apples and starfruit, which are speckled and pulpy and tart. To Grace he gives a pony, and we immediately hate him. Grace and Harry go galloping off to picnics and beach walks and prehistoric sunsets. My father, who himself is surprised to learn he has a brother, disapproves. Without warning, Uncle Harry sets off for Madagascar in search of adventure. As the balloon diminishes against the horizon, we wish him the best (save for Saul, who shoots arrows at the ascension). A month later, Grace disappears. When she finally returns from Tippecanoe, she totes Joshua along with her, a baby in a proverbial basket she rescued from the river. We do not ask questions and Mother adopts the child. Uncle Harry never descends upon us again.

EFFIGY

The death of Sophocles is not the death of Old Yeller. Sophocles never defends us from rabid wolves, never contracts rabies, never is shot by a blubbering boy. Sophocles sleeps the day away and humps furniture and eats us out of house and home. Sophocles' demise blooms deep inside him and doubles in size every week. He smacks his tongue across his black licorice lips and awaits the end. He has bunny dreams and eats peanut butter and grows lethargic. When it is his time to go, we gather 'round to watch death's final act. His tongue undulates like the Chinese dragon on New Year's. The movement hypnotizes all who watch. Once he is gone, we take our ear muffs off. We do not inter Sophocles. We preserve his bulbous corpse with chemical might and keep him as a sturdy doorstop. In the winter we mount his paws to runners and sled down the gulch. When visitors come, we lie and say he was a good dog—the best—and regale them with stories of rescue and valor, of brother Joseph down in the well that would put Lassie to shame. When our house burns down in the winter, the only item we save is Sophocles. We lose everything in the fire but him. Giving thanks, we douse him in kerosene and set him ablaze down the muddy Muscatatuck. Without Sophocles, we start our lives anew.

EARTHQUAKE

WHEN THE EARTH QUAKES, MOTHER BLAMES us for the commotion and sends us to bed without supper. We devise an extravagant plan to recover the lost meal, make dopplegängers in our beds and escape the fortified house by chimney. Soiled, we stow away on a freight train and head west, where hours later we arrive in St. Louis. At the World's Fair, we eat ice cream cones for the first time and hitch a ride on a stagecoach, where disreputable characters tell us soon we'll be men. This proves to be false— we remain six boys and one girl—but in New Orleans, the seven-alarm gumbo puts hair on our chests—even our sister's—so perhaps they were right. There, we meet a steamboat operator heading north and looking for playactors. On board, we appear as the Von Trapp children in a prehistoric rendition of *The Sound of Music*, but our genders are all wrong. We wear drag, go through puberty, and escape Nazis a generation before they invade Poland. We receive a standing ovation. By the time we reach our home, our bellies are full. The earthquake is a distant memory. Our shoulders are broad and our voices deep; we do not recognize ourselves. When we knock on the door, our Mother and Father answer but look at us as strangers. Inside, our dopplegängers sit at the table eating supper. "Can we help you?" our Mother asks. Grace answers on our behalf, "No, ma'am. We must have the wrong address," and we head back to the rails.

CONFESSION

ON HIS DEATH BED, FATHER MAKES A CONFESSION: He hates Mother's lemon meringue. She slaps his dying face and he expires. She serves lemon bars and lemon soup and lemonade at the wake. At the funeral, she grates lemon zest over his pallid face. Everyone puckers when condoling us. No one says he was a sweet man. Mother lines his casket with lemons and tugs his lips into a grin before the undertaker seals the lid. We plant a lemon tree in lieu of headstone, but it dies in the frost. We plant another the next year, but it too dies. For seven years we plant lemon trees that die, until Mother confesses she too hates lemon meringue. We plant a dogwood and ask forgiveness. When she dies, we serve key lime pie and limeade and lime chili. No one calls Mother a sweet woman.

SLEEPWALK

WE ARE A FAMILY OF SLEEPWALKERS. IN THE QUEST for a remedy, one day Father shackles bowling balls to our legs. This solution works until Grace sleep-drags the orb to the second story landing, where velocity sends her hurtling over the edge. The ball crushes her skull at the bottom of the stairs, and after the funeral, Father goes back to the drawing board. "Perhaps an anvil would do the trick." But Peter escapes in the night for a sleep-jog. He sleep-falls into our moat, where he sleep-sleeps with the fishes. We fill the moat in with sand and after the funeral ponder our situation. Father fastens iron manacles to our ankles and wrists. We sleep soundly and snugly. I never sleepwalk again. When a stranger approaches from the forest and knocks on our door, I sleep-speak, "Enter," and she shrieks when she sees us sleep-shackled, peacefully sleep-sleeping. She sits beside me on my bed and spoons piping hot porridge into my mouth. I sleep-eat it and she tells me my bed is too firm. I sleep-agree and never wake up. I sleep-sleep and sleep-sleep and sleep-sleep.

TRANSLATION

BECAUSE SHE DIES AT SEA, WE WEAR DIVING SUITS TO the wake. But because we are beside ourselves, we ask the family mime to eulogize Mother. This, Marcel does in a series of scenic tableaus: delivering happily, sadly, contemplatively, aggressively, and spastically her abbreviated biography. From him we learn there were many stairs Mother climbed, many boats she rowed, and countless ropes she struggled to pull. From within our fish bowls, we sob. It turns out we barely knew her. Marcel neither acknowledges nor denies our prehistoric fear. When my siblings and I ask for a transcript of the eulogy, a colleague to his left renders it in sign language. We do not know sign language, so the stenographer to his left composes it in shorthand. We do not read short hand, so the scholar to his left translates it. When she finishes scribbling the document, we see that it is in Esperanto. We shriek as they must have at the tower of Babel. Her memory is lost to language, her body to the sea. Our tears fill up to the face plate of our helmets, just below our nostrils. We can no longer speak without gurgling salt water. It nearly drowns us.

THE BOOK OF SIN

During his First Reconciliation, Joshua confesses to every sin in the book. Original sin (prehistoric), the ten commandments, the seven deadly sins, mortal sins, venial sins, sins of commission, omission, of thought, and action, sins yet to be committed, and sins without names (posthistoric). After nearly two hours, Father MacCauley sends Joshua on his way with a beginner's penance: ten Hail Marys, one Our Father, and a Glory Be. His slate wiped clean, our brother trots home, where relatives gather to congratulate his exculpation. We bestow on him white rosaries and white handkerchiefs and white doves, which he subsequently loses and soils and maims. The house buzzes with activity. A red-faced Grandpa threatens to spank us bare-bottomed for reasons unknown. Cousins climb in and out of our rooms, hiding-and-seeking-and-touching our genitals without commotion.

Our great aunts carry casseroles from here to there and gossip, call us by the wrong names, and pinch our rosy cheeks. On the television, there is news breaking. Deep within the cathode ray tube, unkempt women project onto the screen. They are walking into the daylight. Their eyes search the newfound world, gauzy and impotent. Their captor, a man who imprisons them in a dungeon for a decade, sits in handcuffs without expression. One of the women stretches her arms out to him. Grace shrugs. "We all suffer from Stockholm syndrome. Except there is no escape from family." We do not question this.

FORT/DA

WHEN WE DIE, WE FIND OURSELVES REUNITED WITH our family. None of us are surprised, except Grace, who takes her afterlife in retaliation, only to reappear a moment later. Because death offers the hope of a final escape, Grace reenacts this disa-reappearance for an eternity. We take wagers on her execution, with each succeeding departure. When she leaves us, Joshua follows like Sophocles. Mother hiccups at the sight. In death, we say all that we could not in life. There are no secrets. Grace never stays long enough to discover this. Wrongdoings are pronounced; grievances aired. All we had longed to know in life is known, but there is no relief. We forget the meaning behind these revelations. We wile away eternity watching our spent lives replay in loops, looking for clues to its meaning, only to find that they are far and few between. The path is winding and impervious, the lives we led foreign films without subtitles. Still, we take in the replay greedily, lapping up every last drop. Our lives never end the way we think they will, but our afterlives carry their routines. In death, we eat marshmallows. Forever hiccuping, Mother roasts them, boils them, fries them, poaches them, sprinkles them with smaller marshmallows, but all in vain. The airy dollops meet our mouths without taste or pleasure. As we chew the cud, a din from some prehistoric space just beyond the fray harkens Grace and Joshua's return. "You're back!" we say, and just as soon, "You're gone!"

WALL DRUG

ON THE ROAD TO TOPEKA MY PARENTS ASK ME WHEN I want to die. My siblings have all vanished by now. We are alone in the car, and it snows heavily. "Soon," I tell them, and they are quiet. The visibility diminishes. We use periscopes to see. When we grow tired, we stop at Wall Drug, where we are accosted by jackalopes; they ravish Mother and browbeat Father. My parents die slowly. The snow falls slowly. I tell them I like them, but the lie prolongs their passing. They ask me when I'm coming, and I say, "Soon." The jackalopes watch along with me, and when it is over, they turn to me, cock their heads, and lick my cowlicked hair. The proprietor gives me a bag of souvenirs, postcards, and a hatchet. He says I can kill the jackalopes—avenge my parents' death—but I do not. I continue driving to Topeka alone. The snow covers the highway in dunes, transporting me to another world.

The earth is prehistoric, but we are not. Families park their cars by the highway and build igloos and snowmen and drink cocoa and pelt each other with violent affection. But I do not. I drive until I am blinded by white. I jump out of the car and let it putter away, taking only the hatchet. Tramping down the vanishing road, I find a derelict farmhouse. Outside it, a camel stands, its tongue extending to catch the frozen flakes. I stare at the camel, and it blinks. I stare at the hatchet, and it glints. I tighten my grip. I know what I must do.

―――
ACKNOWLEDGEMENTS
―――

The following pieces were previously published in these journals:

"Confession," *Redivider*, Spring 2010.

"Malapropos," *Pax Americana*, Spring 2010. (Renamed "Wall Drug")

"Apiarian," "Bingo," and "Translation," *Spring Gun Press*, 1.1, Fall 2009.

"Cat Thrower," *Dogzplot*, May 2009.

ABOUT THE AUTHOR

John Paul Stadler grew up in the wholesome state of Indiana, followed by brief stints in the less-wholesome states of Ohio, Missouri, and Colorado. He currently resides in Durham, North Carolina, where he is completing a doctorate in the Literature Program at Duke University.

ABOUT THE CUPBOARD

The Cupboard is a quarterly pamphlet of creative prose. Each volume features a body of work by a single author. The Cupboard welcomes prose submissions of anywhere between 5,000 and 10,000 words. Submissions can be composed of one piece or multiple pieces. We make no demands on content or genre, with the exception of verse poetry, which we don't publish. We read fiction and nonfiction and are happy to see collections inclusive of both. The Cupboard welcomes submissions from subscribers at any time. Subscribers should submit manuscripts directly to the editors for consideration via email.

To subscribe to The Cupboard, or for more information: www.thecupboardpamphlet.org.